PUFFIN BOOKS

The Worst Witch To The Rescue

Jill Murphy started putting books together (literally with a stapler) when she was six. Her Worst Witch series, the first book of which was published in 1974, is hugely successful. She has also written and illustrated several award-winning picture books for younger children.

Books by Jill Murphy

THE WORST WITCH
THE WORST WITCH STRIKES AGAIN
A BAD SPELL FOR THE WORST WITCH
THE WORST WITCH ALL AT SEA
THE WORST WITCH SAVES THE DAY
THE WORST WITCH TO THE RESCUE
THE WORST WITCH AND THE WISHING STAR

DEAR HOUND

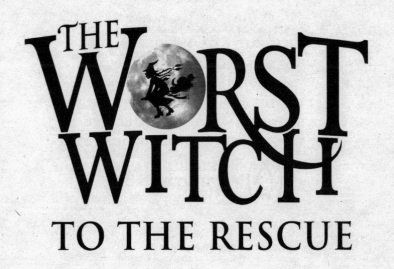

THE WORST WITCH

TO THE RESCUE

JILL MURPHY

PUFFIN

PUFFIN BOOKS

UK | USA | Canada | Ireland | Australia
India | New Zealand | South Africa

Puffin Books is part of the Penguin Random House group of companies
whose addresses can be found at global.penguinrandomhouse.com

www.penguin.co.uk
www.puffin.co.uk
www.ladybird.co.uk

Penguin
Random House
UK

First published 2007
This edition published 2016
002

Copyright © Jill Murphy, 2007

The moral right of the author/illustrator has been asserted

Set in Baskerville
Printed in Great Britain by Clays Ltd, St Ives plc

A CIP catalogue record for this book is available from the British Library

ISBN: 978-0-141-37686-8

All correspondence to:
Puffin Books
Penguin Random House Children's
80 Strand, London WC2R ORL

This book belongs
to

CHAPTER ONE

It was early in the morning on what promised to be a fine day in March, a bit blustery but a perfect start for the first day of Summer Term at Miss Cackle's Academy for Witches.

Dawn had only just broken when a lone figure on a broomstick came swooping and diving through the flocks of early-morning birds, soaring among them with such confidence that from a distance it almost looked like another bird.

The pilot was Ethel Hallow, top student at Miss Cackle's Academy, early as usual and eager to be the first pupil to alight in the schoolyard.

She slowed to an easy pace and hitched her suitcase more securely on to the broom, as it had shifted during a rather ambitious nosedive. Her cat, Nightstar, was wedged between the suitcase and a bundle of box files, one leg in the air, doing some serious washing without a care in the world.

Ethel dropped down a little so that she was skimming the top of the forest which surrounded the academy for several kilometres. She could see the school now, misty on the horizon. There was no one else about, she was sure to be the first – she could take it more slowly from here.

Unusually, Ethel was anxious. The whole class had been set a holiday project and, for once, she hadn't been able to get to grips with it. Normally, the project would involve pupils looking things up in their *Spell Sessions* book and learning some complicated new spell that they hadn't been allowed to tackle before. However, this one was different. Miss Hardbroom, their extremely strict and exacting form mistress, had given them a completely free rein and simply told them to come back with something unusual and interesting.

'That *doesn't* mean you just give it five minutes' consideration on your way back here next term!' Miss Hardbroom had warned them on the last day of the previous term. 'You've all been here long enough, so I'm expecting you to have a little self-motivation and imagination by now.'

Imagination – or the lack of it – was the trouble where Ethel was concerned. It was her only weak point and she found herself in the unheard-of (for her) position of doing exactly what Miss Hardbroom had told them not to do – trying to think up a brilliant project in five minutes flat on the way back to school.

Something caught her eye below and she saw, to her surprise, a tabby cat in

the topmost branches of a beech tree. It miaowed pitifully as she dropped lower and Ethel realized that she could see the top of a school hat, slightly bent, and a figure partly hidden by the tangled branches. That hat! That *cat*! It could only be Mildred Hubble.

'Mildred?' called Ethel, hovering expertly like a helicopter above the little cat's upturned face. 'Is that you down there? Are you OK?'

The hat leaned back, revealing Mildred Hubble's face. 'Oh hi, Ethel,' she said. '*You're* early. I just stopped here for a little rest – well, actually, Tabs fell off and I came down to save him and *then* we stopped for a rest. He's done quite well so far, considering how scared he is of flying. It's so difficult now that we have to keep them on the brooms all the time. Flying was *so* much easier when we could just bung them in their baskets.'

'Easier for *you*, you mean,' said Ethel, hovering down through the branches until she found a space next to Mildred. 'Nightstar was just born to fly. She was brilliant from day one.'

'Hmm,' mumbled Mildred. 'Yes, well, you've always been the lucky one, Ethel. It wasn't my fault I was given Tabby – though he's got a lovely nature and he's the perfect pet, even if he *can't* do anything else.'

Ethel arranged her broom and luggage carefully behind a cluster of branches which grew from the trunk like a giant upturned hand.

'Budge up,' she said, sitting down next to Mildred. 'What's that in your cat basket?' she asked, peering inside the basket, where there was definitely something lurking at the far end.

'Oh – er – nothing!' said Mildred brightly. 'Just some bits and pieces I couldn't fit into my suitcase. The cat basket was empty for the flight, so I thought I'd use it for extra stuff – you know. How did you get on with the holiday project by the way?' she added, swiftly changing the subject.

'Ah, yes,' said Ethel, 'the holiday project. Well, it was quite a challenge, wasn't it? How did *you* get on?'

A shy smile spread over Mildred's face. 'Quite well, as a matter of fact,' she replied. 'I had a *really* good idea. In fact, it was the best idea I've ever had in my whole life! Then I looked up all the relevant bits in an ancient spell book in our local library. It's an amazing old book, tiny print – you actually need a magnifying glass – and hardly any pictures, so it's a bit boring, but it's got everything in it. Anyway, I've got it all written down, so for once I can't wait to get to school and show everyone. Makes a change, eh?'

'What exactly *is* the spell?' asked Ethel casually.

'Well,' said Mildred proudly, 'it isn't actually a known spell. I sort of made it up by myself. It's to make an animal able to speak. Not like when a human turns into an animal, because, when that happens, the human sort of *becomes* the animal and can talk as the animal would. No, this is to make a small animal under twenty-five centimetres square able to have a conversation with a person. The animal has to be a maximum size because you have to make an exact formula for a particular body area – which means that it has to be correct down to the last detail. I tried to get it bigger, because I was dying to have a chat with Tabby, but I couldn't get the equation right for the larger size, so I gave up trying. Anyway, I've actually managed to work it all out for twenty-five centimetres and under –

all the incantations, and the herbs and how to mix it – so you could have a chat with, say, a toad or a field mouse. Oh, and it only works for two weeks on each animal and after those two weeks you can never get it to speak again. Weird, isn't it?'

'How do you know it only lasts for two weeks?' asked Ethel, intrigued. 'I mean, if *you* invented the spell, how do you *know*?'

Mildred smiled.

'Well, actually I *have* tried it,' she said. 'I tried it on a shrew and a young hedgehog and a newt, who all fitted the size criterion – I don't know *why* I'm telling you all this, Ethel, I expect your project is a zillion times more interesting.'

Ethel did her best to look admiring and pleased for Mildred.

'Gosh, Mildred,' she enthused, 'you really have come up with a winner there. My idea's *nothing* compared with that. What did the shrew and the hedgehog *say*?'

'Not much actually,' said Mildred. 'The hedgehog was quite quiet and shy, just asked if it could have a saucer of water and be directed to the nearest slug-infested flowerbed, but the shrew was

really quite nasty – very bad-tempered and complaining about everything. I was glad when the two weeks were up and it suddenly went back to squeaking.

I noticed that both of them stopped being able to talk bang on fourteen days at noon and that, however hard I tried, I couldn't get them speaking again. So I used the formula on a newt and it worked, though newts aren't very chatty either – just for two weeks again, so it's been properly tested. I've written it all up and put it in this special folder. Look, fifteen pages! H.B. won't believe it until she sees how well it works.' She held up a neat blue folder.

Mildred suddenly felt slightly uneasy, sitting there in a tree with Ethel, having what appeared to be a normal, pleasant conversation. Up until this point the two girls had never had any conversation longer than two minutes without an argument developing.

'Come on then,' she said, putting the folder back into her school bag and beginning to gather her things together. 'We'd better set off or we'll be late after our early start. Thanks for listening, Ethel. I must admit I'm quite proud of myself, for once.'

'And with very good reason,' Ethel said, smiling. 'It's an excellent idea. I wish I'd thought of it myself.'

As they pulled themselves up on the branches, gathering their cats and bags, Ethel lurched sideways, knocking Mildred's overstuffed school bag. It was still unfastened and everything went tumbling down through the branches in a cascade of pages and folders. At

the same time, her pencil tin flipped open and her twenty brand-new sharp-pointed coloured pencils clink-clinked down the tree, bouncing through the twigs and buds.

'Oh no!' exclaimed Mildred as Tabby scrabbled further up the tree, miaowing with fright at the commotion.

'Don't worry, Mildred,' said Ethel. 'You grab Tabby and I'll pick everything up for you.'

Ethel climbed down the tree, painstakingly picking up all the paperwork and the pencils and carefully putting everything back into the bag.

'I'm so sorry not to help,' called Mildred. 'I'm trying to keep hold of Tabby or he'll be off and I'll never find him up here. Have you got everything?'

'*Nearly* everything!' called Ethel, who was out of sight at the base of the tree. 'How many coloured pencils were there?'

'Twenty!' called Mildred.

'Hang on!' Ethel shouted. 'They're scattered all over the place.'

For several minutes, Mildred heard Ethel rustling about in the bushes, then it went quiet. 'Are you all right, Ethel?' she called, holding on tightly to the struggling Tabby.

'Yep!' called Ethel. 'Got the very last one – the red one! Coming right back up now!'

Ethel appeared through the branches with the bag across her shoulder and Mildred could see that it was nicely full, with the precious blue folder slightly sticking out between books and exercise books. Ethel patted everything neatly down into the bag and fastened the straps. 'There you go!' she said, handing it over, sounding really glad to have helped.

'Thanks so much, Ethel,' said Mildred. 'This is such a great way to start a new term, isn't it?'

'Isn't it *just*!' said Ethel. 'Come on, race you to school!'

CHAPTER TWO

By the time Ethel and Mildred had rearranged their belongings and launched themselves from a suitable cluster of branches, the morning was well under way and little knots of pupils could be seen converging on the school from all directions.

'You don't mind if I zoom on ahead, do you?' asked Ethel. 'I'm sorry, it's just that you *are* still a bit slower than me.'

'Of *course* I don't mind,' said Mildred cheerily. 'Thanks for helping when I dropped everything.'

'Don't mention it,' said Ethel, who shot off like a bullet and was out of sight in seconds.

Mildred bobbed along slowly towards the school feeling delightfully light-hearted. She could hardly wait to see the class turn in their seats, gazing up at her with admiration as she read out her well-researched notes, then gave a demonstration of how the spell worked. Best of all, she imagined the expression on Miss Hardbroom's face, unsure at first, then fascinated and finally deeply impressed as she realized how hard the worst witch in school had been working during the holidays and how much she had improved.

The school bell began to clang in the distance and Mildred urged the broomstick on as fast as she dared, with Tabby yowling on the back.

'Hang on, Tab,' she called over her shoulder. 'Nearly there now. Gosh, I can hardly wait!'

Mildred almost literally bumped into Maud and Enid, her two closest friends, as they approached the school, which rose up ahead of them in the most sinister way, like a cross between a castle and a top-security prison. Mildred looked upwards at the seemingly endless grey stone walls, which blotted out the sunny sky, and headed for the schoolyard wall.

'Hey, Mildred!' yelled Maud, waving enthusiastically. 'Over here.'

'Hi, Milly!' called Enid. 'Here we are again.'

'Great to see you,' said Mildred, putting a protective hand behind her

to keep Tabby firmly in place as they hovered down the wall on the other side and landed among the throng of pupils.

All around there was a loud hum of voices chatting, laughing, calling out to friends and exchanging tales of the holidays.

'So, what's new?' asked Mildred, sitting down on her suitcase and giving Tabby a calming cuddle.

'I had a holiday job most of the time,' said Enid. 'Fixing handles on cauldrons at a cauldron-maker's. It's a bit like a blacksmith's, but of course I wasn't allowed to do any of the interesting work at the furnace – health and safety, you know. I just did the fiddly bits, fitting the handles – *very* fiddly on the smaller ones for schools. It was grim really – incredibly hot and hardly *any* pay – but I managed to save up a bit for the summer hols. What about you, Maud?'

'Oh, nothing much,' said Maud. 'Just being at home and trying to come up with something good for the holiday project – NOT! Couldn't think of anything stupendous, though. In the end I just rehashed an old spell from *Year Three Spell Sessions*. H.B.'s bound to notice where it really came from. How about *you*, Mil? What did *you* come up with?'

Mildred beamed at her friends.

'You'll just have to wait and see,' she said mysteriously.

'Oh, go on, Mil,' said Enid. 'What is it?'

'*Do* tell,' agreed Maud.

'Nope,' laughed Mildred. 'I'm unveiling my project to the world at the proper moment. That is, when we have the first potions lesson this afternoon. All I *will* say is – prepare to be astounded!'

After that, neither Maud nor Enid could get another word on the subject out of their friend and soon they were busy unpacking their clothes and going down to breakfast, followed by assembly.

Usually, they all met up in Mildred's room for a quick chat before the first lesson, but Mildred was being uncharacteristically secretive. At one point, Maud opened Mildred's door to see if she had five minutes to spare and found Mildred muttering into the cat basket. She obviously wasn't chatting

to Tabby, because the little striped cat was draped around her shoulders in his usual position, like a shawl. Mildred jumped up as soon as she heard the door open.

'What?' she asked, sounding flustered.

'Sorry,' said Maud. 'I just wondered if you were free for a little natter. What's in the basket, Mil?'

'Basket?' asked Mildred. 'Oh – *that* basket. Nothing. Why?'

'You were *talking* into the basket,' said Maud, 'and it obviously isn't Tabby.'

'Oh, *that*,' said Mildred. 'Er, yes, well, I was just practising the words to that new chant. I keep getting them muddled up.'

Maud looked at Mildred, eyes slightly narrowed.

'And there's some extra stuff from home in the basket,' Mildred blundered on. 'I sort of used it as an extra suitcase for the journey – there's the bell!' she exclaimed, sounding heartily relieved. 'See you in the art room, Maud. It's *pottery*. What a brill way to start a new term.'

CHAPTER THREE

Maud and Enid made their way up one of the winding staircases which led to the art room.

'She's up to something,' said Maud anxiously.

'Who?' asked Enid.

'*Mildred*, of course,' said Maud. 'I just know there's something funny going on. She's *hiding* something in her cat basket and pretending she isn't.'

'Perhaps you imagined it,' said Enid hopefully.

'Imagined what?' called Mildred, who had dashed up the stairs behind them.

'Um – I imagined that I saw Ethel being nice to one of the first-years,' laughed Maud.

'That wouldn't surprise me actually,' said Mildred. 'I met her on the way in and she was *really* nice.'

'Perhaps she's been on a "niceness course",' suggested Enid. 'She always takes about three hundred courses during the hols.'

They all giggled as they trooped into the art room, which was Mildred's favourite room in the school. There was a row of hooks from which hung dozens of overalls and the girls took one each and struggled into them before they sat down. The room was very large, with stone walls and slit windows, exactly like all the other rooms in the school, with a wooden picture rail all the way around so that framed pictures and the pupils' drawings and paintings could be displayed, and a double sink with draining boards along one wall. At the far end was an empty space for the girls to work on sculptures. The rest of the room was full of tables and chairs. The teacher's desk was on a raised wooden platform with two steps up to it and sitting at the desk was Miss Mould, the new teacher.

Miss Mould looked surprisingly normal for a teacher at Miss Cackle's Academy. She had short mousy hair, parted in the centre and pulled into a ponytail at her neck, where it was secured by a black velvet bow. Her black skirt was topped by a grey twinset and a neat row of black pearls. Her voice was soft and kindly, a welcome change from Miss Hardbroom's crisp way of speaking and certainly a great relief after the extremely weird Miss Granite, who had caused such chaos the term before.

Mildred felt a tiny flicker of disappointment that Miss Mould wasn't more arty-looking, but apart from that she seemed quite pleasant.

'Good morning, Form Three,' said Miss Mould with a shy smile.

'Good *morning*, Miss Mould,' chorused the girls, who were now standing behind their tables.

'You may sit,' said Miss Mould. 'I was slightly dismayed,' she continued, 'to find that there is hardly any equipment for pottery at Miss Cackle's Academy. Ceramics is my favourite subject and I was looking forward to passing on my skills to you all. I think art has been a little *basic* here until now, but Miss Cackle has promised me a second room with enough potters' wheels for everyone *and* a kiln if we can show a real aptitude for the subject this term. So, let's try and make master craftsmen – or should I say women! – of you all. What do you say, girls?'

It was not the sort of school where anyone dared to shout 'YESSSS!', so Form Three just smiled and mumbled in agreement.

'Right,' said Miss Mould with enthusiasm, heaving a huge sack of wet clay from behind the desk. 'I want you all to take a lump of clay – enough to hold in both hands – back to your desks. *Dig* your fingers in and *scoop* it out. Don't be *afraid* of the clay, girls! *Feel* the *squishiness* of it, get it under your nails. That's it, *scoop* it out, *knead* it. Bring that clay to life! Become one with the clay!'

The girls exchanged amused glances at the flowery language as they formed a queue and then each pulled themselves a dollop of clay which they took back to their tables. Meanwhile, Miss Mould had distributed bowls of water to each table so that they could keep their work damp to avoid the clay drying out. There was a wooden board, a set of sculpting tools and a rolling pin, neatly laid out at each place.

Miss Mould showed them how to make coil pots, which involved rolling out thin sausages of clay and stacking them on top of each other. They could then smooth the coils into each other to make a substantial pot.

Mildred felt almost hysterical with hope about the way her new term was progressing. First of all, she had a superb project with which to amaze Miss Hardbroom that afternoon. Then there was Ethel being so friendly on the way to school – she hadn't once sneered about Tabby or about Mildred dropping her bag, and had even helped to pick everything up. Now there was a new teacher for a subject that Mildred enjoyed and was actually good at. By the end of the day she might have gold stars all over her personal chart and be in line for a merit badge at the end of the week. With joy in her heart, Mildred plunged her fingers into the squelchy lump and became one with the clay.

CHAPTER FOUR

For a while there was very little sound as everyone concentrated on their task. First of all they rolled the clay flat with little rolling pins, then they cut clay bases for the coils to sit on.

'It's just like cookery,' said Enid.

Next they set about making their rolls of clay. Mildred made hers especially thin and laid them out in neat rows, deliberately grading them in length so that she could narrow them on the way up the pot to make an interesting shape.

Miss Mould wandered among the tables, keeping an eye on proceedings. She stopped and looked over Mildred's shoulder.

'What is your name?' she asked.

'Mildred Hubble,' replied Mildred nervously.

'Have you done this before?' asked Miss Mould.

'No, Miss Mould,' said Mildred. 'But I have made lots of things out of shoeboxes and cotton reels. I do like making things.'

Miss Mould wandered around the rest of the class, giving the odd word of encouragement and examining the girls' progress. After a while, she stepped back on to the platform and clapped her hands.

'Listen a moment, girls,' she said. 'I'd like you all to go and take a look at Mildred Hubble's work. She seems to be a real natural at pottery and you could all benefit from seeing how neatly she has arranged and graded her coils.'

Mildred blushed with delight and Maud nudged her proudly under the table.

'*Un*fortunately,' continued Miss Mould, 'some of you are positively *un*natural when it comes to clay – that girl at the back, for instance. What is your name?'

Ethel realized with horror that Miss Mould was gesturing in her direction. She glanced sideways, hoping it might be her friend Drusilla, who was sitting next to her. In fact, Drusilla couldn't believe it either and pointed at her own chest, mouthing 'Me?'

'No, dear,' said Miss Mould. 'That girl next to you with the ponytail and the black hair ribbon. What is your name?'

Ethel stood up, seething inwardly. 'Ethel Hallow,' she said clearly, with a defiant toss of the ponytail.

'Ethel,' said Miss Mould, 'your coils look as if they've been made by a three-year-old. They're *much* too short and too fat – your pot would be only two centimetres in diameter if, in fact, you could get the coils to bend without cracking. Perhaps Mildred could change places with the girl next to you and give you a hand. In fact, change places now, then the class can file past and see the two examples next to each other.'

Mildred and Drusilla changed places, carefully lifting their boards containing the rolls of clay and the remaining clay lump. Ethel was sending out an invisible, almost electric, current of rage as Mildred took the place next to her and everyone began filing past.

'Sorry, Ethel,' mumbled Mildred, not wishing to ruin their good start. 'Your coils aren't *that* bad, they're just a bit short.'

'Shut up, Mildred Hubble!' snapped Ethel under her breath. 'I don't need *you* to teach me anything.'

'Sorry,' said Mildred in an even smaller voice.

Form Three settled down again and Mildred tried to forget Ethel, vibrating with rage next to her, as she began arranging the coils one by one on top of each other.

Ethel suddenly leaned across. 'Sorry, Mildred,' she said, much to Mildred's surprise. 'I didn't mean to bite your head off. Look – are these a bit better? I've tried to make them thinner – like yours.'

Mildred gave a nervous smile.

'They're *much* better,' she said, grateful that Ethel had pulled herself together.

'Could you cut the ends like yours,' said Ethel, 'so they're just a bit smaller each time? Mine get sort of squashed when I try to do them.'

'Of *course*,' said Mildred, a wave of relief sweeping over her that Ethel had not nosedived into a full-blown feud, as she usually did if the tiniest thing upset her.

'Let's change places for a mo,' said Ethel. 'I can study the way you're building up your coils while you grade my ends for me.'

'OK,' said Mildred. 'Move up then.'

Ethel sat gazing intently at Mildred's pot. She picked up the four remaining

coils, passing them very carefully through her fingers, then delicately held the half-completed pot in both hands.

'I think I've got the hang of it now,' she said.

'That's great,' said Mildred. 'I've graded your coils for you.'

They changed places again and Ethel put a friendly hand on Mildred's shoulder. 'You really *are* good, Milly,' she said. 'Your pot will make everyone sit up and take notice, just you wait and see.'

CHAPTER FIVE

Miss Mould looked up from her desk.

'Whoever is making that noise,' she said sharply, 'would they please stop it.'

The hum of conversation had dwindled to a standstill as the pupils had begun concentrating in earnest. Now everyone looked around as they tuned into the noise that Miss Mould had mentioned. She was right. There was a definite noise, which came in a burst every few seconds, then stopped abruptly. It sounded as if somebody had hidden a maraca from the school orchestra cupboard and was shaking it under a table. The noise stopped.

Everyone strained their ears, but it didn't happen again.

'Thank you,' said Miss Mould crisply.

Mystified, the girls went back to their coils, all except Mildred, who felt distinctly uneasy as the strange rattling noise seemed to be coming directly from her table. She dropped her smoothing

tool on purpose and bent down to pick it up so that she could check beneath the table, but there was nothing there except a piece of ancient chewing gum. The noise started again and this time it seemed to be directly *above* her. It went on for longer, becoming insistent, almost angry, and as Mildred raised her head there was a piercing scream from Ethel.

Mildred cracked her head on the table as she jumped up and found herself face to face with the most terrifying sight she had ever seen. The coil pot was no longer a neat pile of damp clay coils. It was a rattlesnake, quivering its awful tail as a warning, its head pulled back as if to strike. Crouched behind the table was Ethel, white as a sheet, her mouth still open as her scream died away. The other four clay coils had turned into four smaller rattlesnakes, growing larger by the minute. They all slithered to the edge of the table and arranged themselves in a hissing, spitting row, lunging forward every so often and striking the air.

As soon as the girls saw what was happening on Mildred and Ethel's table, there was pandemonium.

'Quickly, girls!' yelled Miss Mould, who could scarcely believe her eyes. '*Move!*'

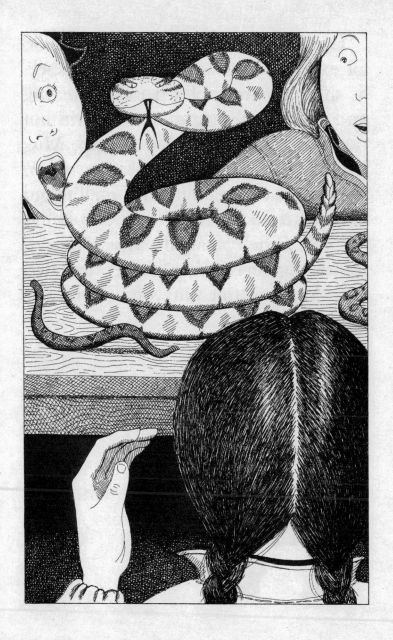

Everyone stampeded for the door, all except Ethel, who stopped as soon as she had two tables between herself and the ghastly sight of the writhing rattlesnakes. 'I think I can help, Miss Mould,' she called across the room. 'I'm sure I can remember a spell to get rid of them.'

'No, Ethel!' called Miss Mould, frantically beckoning Ethel towards her. 'You mustn't put yourself in any danger!'

'I'll just *try*, Miss Mould,' called Ethel. 'They can't be allowed to escape.'

Ethel turned and faced the snakes across the tables. She raised her arms high above her head to keep her hands as far away as possible, flexing her fingers towards them and murmuring a spell very softly in a pulsing tone. There was a zigzag flash, followed by a loud crack and smoke which smelled like gunpowder. As the smoke began to clear, the image of the snakes hung for a

few seconds in the air, then disintegrated and vaporized so that nothing was left of them at all.

At Ethel and Mildred's table, Ethel's clay coils were where she had left them, but Mildred's half-made pot and the remaining coils were blown apart in jagged lumps, with bits of clay spattered up the walls and all over Mildred's chair.

Miss Mould stood gaping by the door. Most of the pupils were already in the corridor, but they all craned their necks around Miss Mould to see into the art room. Apart from Ethel, Mildred was

the only other pupil still there, near the doorway.

Ethel turned around with a beaming smile. 'Just as well I studied *that* one for fun during the hols,' she said triumphantly. 'It's all right, Miss Mould – it was only a simple blasting spell called Smithereens. They won't come back now.'

Miss Mould ushered Form Three back into the room and gathered them together in the sculpture space while she examined the table to make sure it was safe. Mildred was shocked to the core. It was *her* pot that had done this and she had absolutely no idea why.

On cue, Miss Hardbroom was suddenly standing in the doorway.

'Oh, Miss Hardbroom!' exclaimed Miss Mould. 'Thank *goodness* you're here. Mildred Hubble's coil pot suddenly turned into a *nest* of snakes and if Ethel hadn't been quick off the mark I fear there would have been a very serious incident indeed.'

Miss Hardbroom fixed Mildred with her laser-beam glare.

'Mildred Hubble,' she said, icily calm. 'Why is this no surprise to me?'

'I-I-I,' was all Mildred could manage. 'I – it – I don't – it wasn't – I never –'

'Stop *wittering*, Mildred!' barked Miss Hardbroom. 'I suppose this is your idea of livening things up a bit, putting your classmates in mortal danger. What on *earth* were you thinking of? Thank goodness Ethel has such school spirit. It was extremely brave of you, Ethel, to take on – what were they, Miss Mould?'

'Five rattlesnakes, Miss Hardbroom,' said Miss Mould faintly.

'*Five rattlesnakes!*' exclaimed Miss Hardbroom. 'This is worse than I thought. Obviously pottery is a subject fraught with danger for everyone else while you are in the class, Mildred! You'd better have extra lessons on classroom etiquette with me for the rest of term or Miss Mould will find herself in charge of a zoo. Go to your room for the rest of the lesson, while I help to get this class back to some semblance of normality.'

Mildred stood transfixed, still shocked.

'Now!' ordered Miss Hardbroom.

Mildred turned and barged past her classmates, catching a fleeting glimpse of the horrified faces of Maud and Enid as she raced away from all the commotion and out into the cool stone corridor.

CHAPTER SIX

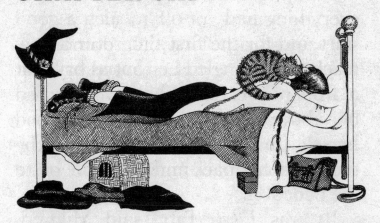

Tabby, who was asleep on Mildred's pillow, was nearly flattened as Mildred hurled herself on to her narrow iron bedstead, sobbing as if her heart would break. Tabby had jumped out of the way on to the window sill, but he soon realized that his mistress was upset and busied himself twining around her head, leaning against her, chirruping and purring, and eventually giving up and sitting squarely on her back, purring like a car engine.

She had been so *happy* for once – everything had got off to such a good start and for the first time ever a new teacher had singled her out as brilliant in front of everyone. She'd even praised her above Ethel. Ethel! Mildred raised herself up on her elbows and Tabby slid down her back and rolled off on to the bedcover.

'It was *Ethel*, Tab,' said Mildred, sitting up and knuckling her eyes. 'Ethel did it, when she asked to hold my pot and feel all the coils. She was casting a spell on them. I might have known Ethel wouldn't have truly been interested in anything *I'd* done. Oh, Tabby, it wasn't *my* fault Miss Mould liked my work better – and now everyone thinks it was me who conjured up those awful snakes.'

Mildred took off her overall, got into the bed and pulled the covers right up to her eyes. Tabby was very pleased about this and nestled into the pillow around the top of her head. She wished she had managed to sort out a speaking spell for larger animals, then Tabby could have actually held a conversation with her. On the other hand, it would have been terrible when it ended forever after two weeks and, come to think of it, he virtually *did* speak to her with all his nudging and purring. He had the most soothing purr, loud and constant, a sort of massage for the mind.

She tried concentrating on the positive aspects of her situation – not that she could think of many. It was *sort* of positive that she hadn't been expelled on the spot; it was *very* positive that potions was the first lesson after lunch, so she had the perfect chance to redeem herself when Miss Hardbroom asked them to present their holiday projects. She glanced across at the blue folder lying proudly on top of her pile of school books.

'At least I've still got *you*,' she said to herself, blowing a kiss across the room.

Someone tapped lightly on the door. Mildred didn't answer, afraid it might be Ethel come to gloat.

'Mildred?' She heard Maud's voice. 'Are you in there? It's me – and Enid. Can we come in?'

Mildred climbed out of the bed and opened the door.

'All right,' she said. 'I'm surprised

you're brave enough to come anywhere near me. I don't suppose you'll believe me if I tell you it was Ethel.'

'What on earth happened?' asked Enid. 'How do you *know* it was Ethel?'

'Well, it certainly wasn't *me*,' said Mildred. 'Didn't you notice how furious Ethel was when Miss Mould liked my stuff better than hers?'

'Not really,' said Enid.

'I thought she took it rather well,' said Maud. 'When I looked across, she was chatting to you and examining your stuff. I thought Drusilla took it worse than she did.'

'Yes, well,' said Mildred, 'that was all just a cover-up. She was *really* putting a spell on my pot, though I must admit, from the look on her face, I don't think she knew they were going to be *deadly* snakes. Perhaps she thought they'd be fake ones or something. Anyway, here I go again. First morning and everything's gone pear-shaped.'

Maud sat down next to Mildred and found herself looking at the cat basket, which was half hidden under a heap of towels and nightclothes.

'Aren't you going to tell us what you've got in the cat basket, Mil?' she asked. 'I know you're hiding something.'

'Perhaps it's a boa constrictor!' laughed Enid. 'Sorry, Mil, I know you didn't do it – just a joke.'

'If I tell you what it is,' said Mildred, 'you mustn't tell anyone else.'

'Promise,' said Maud and Enid together.

Mildred pulled the basket out and put it on to the bed.

'OK,' she said. 'It's a tortoise.'

CHAPTER SEVEN

'A tortoise!' exclaimed Maud. 'Why on *earth* have you brought a tortoise to school?'

'H.B. will have a brainstorm if she sees it,' said Enid. 'You *know* we can't have any other pets except the cats.'

'And bats, if any are roosting in the room,' Maud reminded them, 'but that's *it*. Bats and cats. End of story.'

Mildred opened the wire door of the cat basket and brought out the surprise occupant, a sleeping tortoise. All they could see was the brown shell and the cave-like holes at the front and back where it had retracted itself.

'He won't be any trouble,' explained Mildred. 'He can trundle about in my room during the day when I'm at lessons and he only eats fruit and vegetables, so I can sneak stuff from the dining hall. Now they've all gone mad on healthy school dinners there's a bowl of fruit and salad stuff on every table and there's always loads left. He's called Speedy.'

'Oh, *Mildred*!' said Maud wearily. 'Why do you always set yourself up for disaster? Something's *bound* to happen with a tortoise – A TORTOISE, for heaven's sake!'

'And *we* believe you about the snakes, Milly,' said Enid. 'But H.B. won't and there's no way you can prove it was Ethel, especially as she was being nice.'

'*Pretending* to be nice!' Mildred corrected.

'Pretending to be nice then,' agreed Enid, 'but that scream wasn't put on. Ethel sounded as freaked out as everyone else.'

'Only because she didn't realize the snakes were going to be quite so horrible,' grumbled Mildred.

'*Look*, Mil,' said Maud, beginning to sound faintly irritated. 'We're just going round in circles here. *We* believe you. OK? You don't have to prove anything to us – we're your best friends – but keep your head down now and perhaps H.B. will relent on her pottery ban when she sees your super-duper holiday project.'

'What made you want a tortoise in the first place?' asked Enid. 'They don't *do* much and you've never said anything about tortoises before.'

'I can't tell you yet,' said Mildred, 'but I promise I'll tell you very soon.'

'Is it to do with the holiday project?' asked Maud.

'*Sort of*,' said Mildred with a secret smile.

Mildred put Speedy back into the basket as he was still fast asleep and the three friends set off to the dining hall.

Lunch was supposed to be chicken and vegetable pie, but the pastry was like concrete (Mildred actually bent her knife trying to cut it) and there was only a small puddle of gravy inside after all the hard work of hacking through like a mining operation.

To make matters worse, the story of the rattlesnake incident had spread through the school like wildfire and everyone was calling out rude remarks and making jokes at Mildred's expense. She tried to laugh it off good-naturedly at first, but after a while her eyes filled with tears.

'Glad to ssssee you ssssurvived, Mildred,' hissed Drusilla as she passed by, carrying pudding for herself and Ethel.

'Don't take any notice,' said Maud soothingly.

'Anyway, it's nearly time to reveal your holiday project,' said Enid. 'That'll show everyone.'

'Hey, Mildred!' called Ethel from the next table. 'Ssssyrup ssssponge and cussssstard for afterssss!'

Mildred got up and pushed back her chair. 'I'll see you later,' she said to Maud and Enid. 'I can't stand any more of this.'

Blushing furiously, she hurried through the gauntlet of laughter, back to the peace of her room. Speedy was still fast asleep, so Mildred laid some carrot sticks and celery in the cat basket in front of him in case he woke up feeling hungry. Then she picked up the blue folder containing the precious holiday project and sat on the edge of her bed, holding it against her chest, feeling tempted to have one last look.

She had been so worried she might mislay a page or, worse, put the whole thing down somewhere and lose it completely that she hadn't opened the folder since she had packed it ready to take to school.

Maud and Enid knocked at her door.

'Come on, Mil!' said Maud cheerily. 'Time for your big moment. Potions with H.B. and the best holiday project in the world.'

'Well, perhaps not in the *world*,' said Mildred, smiling.

'Don't start being modest *now*,' said Enid. 'We're expecting to be greatly impressed.'

'Greatly impressed you certainly will be,' said Mildred. 'Come on, let's go and make H.B.'s day!'

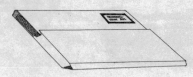

CHAPTER EIGHT

Miss Hardbroom was already seated at her desk in the potion laboratory with an all-knowing look on her face as Form Three filed in and took their places at their workbenches. She had an unpleasant knack of making every pupil feel that they might have done something wrong, even if they hadn't – although in Mildred's case there was usually some backlog of disasters, such as the snake incident, causing Miss Hardbroom to keep a close eye on her.

This time Mildred could hardly wait to smooth things over by revealing the evidence of her hard work during the holidays.

'Good afternoon, girls,' said Miss Hardbroom. 'This is always my favourite day of the whole term. Here you are, all rested and eager to improve your minds with another term of concentration and hard work, anxious to show your worthiness to be in a school as excellent as Miss Cackle's Academy.'

Mildred gazed at Miss Hardbroom in awe. She was never sure if the terrifying teacher was joking when she gave them these little pep talks (which she did at least twice a day).

Surely even Miss Hardbroom couldn't think that they were truly eager to rush back to lessons and concrete pie after a blissful holiday at home wearing their own clothes, eating normal food and doing whatever they wanted?

'Now then,' continued Miss Hardbroom, 'holiday projects! Which one of you would like to be the first to entertain us?'

Ethel shot up a hand before anyone else had a chance.

'*I* will, Miss Hardbroom,' she said with a confident smile, brandishing a purple ring-binder. 'Shall I bring it up to your desk or would you like me to read it aloud myself?'

'Read it yourself, Ethel,' said Miss Hardbroom. 'You always read with such expression.'

Ethel held up the ring-binder and began to read. 'During the holidays, I decided to invent a spell that had never been attempted before, as far as I know. It was a spell to make an animal speak. To do this I had to assemble various components of the spell, including chants, herbs etc., and to make things easier I decided to concentrate on animals which would fit into a space of twenty-five centimetres square and under. I could then formulate the correct amounts of all the ingredients for animals up to that size . . .'

Mildred's jaw dropped as Ethel's voice droned on, reading out word for word the spell which Mildred had spent the entire holiday researching and trying out. When Ethel got to the part where she had looked up everything in an ancient spell book at her local library with a magnifying glass, Mildred could stand it no longer and leapt up, pushing back her stool so forcefully that it fell over.

'Ethel!' she exclaimed furiously. 'What on earth are you doing? That's *my* spell!'

Ethel looked helplessly at Miss Hardbroom. 'I don't know what she's *talking* about, Miss Hardbroom,' she said, sounding alarmed and upset at the same time.

'*Well*, Mildred,' snapped Miss Hardbroom, 'what *are* you talking about? You surely don't imagine that anyone in their right mind would believe that you could possibly have put in the amount of work needed to assemble – how many pages, Ethel?'

'Fifteen,' simpered Ethel.

'Fifteen pages of a holiday project,' continued Miss Hardbroom, 'that obviously required a sharp brain, superb concentration and unbelievable patience. I don't remember you ever displaying even one of these worthy characteristics, Mildred.'

'But I *did*, Miss Hardbroom,' spluttered Mildred, blushing bright red with embarrassment as the whole class turned to look at her. 'Look! It's all here in my folder.'

Miss Hardbroom gestured in a highly irritated fashion for Mildred to bring the folder up to her desk. Mildred watched as she opened it, drew out the pages and looked through them. The glance she shot at Mildred was so angry that Mildred was suddenly gripped by panic.

'Is this your idea of a *joke*, Mildred?' thundered Miss Hardbroom. She turned the pages around and held them up one by one for the class to see. On each page was a smiley face drawn in a different-coloured pencil.

Mildred was so shocked that she couldn't speak.

'*Well*, Mildred?' raged Miss Hardbroom. 'They're not even *good* drawings and they certainly don't represent hours of invention and concentration, which was the whole *point* of this project.' She suddenly deflated and sounded tired. 'Oh, go to your room, Mildred, for the rest of the lesson – again. Perhaps you could stay there for the rest of the *term* with that dreadful cat, while we all have some fun with Ethel's fascinating idea.

'Have you tried it out on any animals, Ethel?' she asked, turning back to Ethel, who was poised to continue.

'Yes, Miss Hardbroom,' said Ethel earnestly, 'there was a hedgehog, a shrew and a newt, but I've brought along a toad so we can try it out during the lesson.'

Mildred burst into tears.

'Are you still *here*, Mildred Hubble?' barked Miss Hardbroom. 'Perhaps I could help you along.'

In front of the whole class, Miss

Hardbroom muttered the words to a transference spell and Mildred found herself hurtling through a tunnel of air and whirling lights and hurled, as if she had been shot from a cannon, on to her bed, nearly flattening Tabby for the second time in one day.

CHAPTER NINE

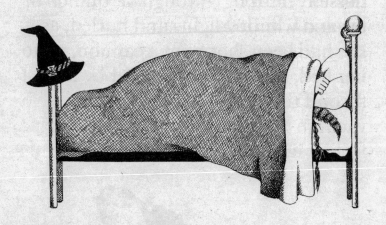

Deep beneath the bedcovers, Mildred had curled herself up in a ball, too shocked and upset even to cry any more. Tabby had got right inside the bedclothes with her and was lending his support by purring at the top of his purr and passionately kneading her with tiny claw-prickles as he flexed his paws against her arms.

To be 'transferred' was the most humiliating dismissal a teacher could possibly make. It was an even more insulting version of an adult saying, 'Get out of my sight.' Apart from the unpleasantness of being instantly pulled through a void as if by an invisible vacuum cleaner, it left the recipient feeling unceremoniously got rid of and swatted like an irritating bluebottle.

The bright new day had collapsed around Mildred's ears as though she had walked into a line full of wet washing, and the more she thought about what had happened, the more weighed down and tangled up she felt. It all came back to her: the conversation with Ethel in the tree, where she had told Ethel every single detail of her wonderful idea, and the 'accident' when Mildred's bag had fallen to the ground, followed by Ethel 'helping', taking ages to pick up all Mildred's things – picking them up and switching Mildred's project for a stack of empty paper.

As the hours dragged by, Mildred heard the bell for each change of lesson and finally the five long bells to signify the end of the school day. She rather hoped that Maud and Enid would come to commiserate with her, as they usually did, but half an hour later there was still no sign of them.

Just when she had given up listening out, there was a soft tap and Maud and Enid looked nervously round the edge of the door.

'We've brought you some tea,' said Enid. 'It's a scone –'

'– or a rock cake,' said Maud. 'It's hard to tell which – and a cup of tea.'

'Thanks,' said Mildred gratefully. 'I don't know whether H.B. expects me to stay here for the rest of my life or what.'

'If I were you, I'd just keep out of the way tonight,' said Maud. 'She'll be over it by the morning.'

'Watch out,' said Mildred, jumping off the bed and diving for Speedy, who was plodding determinedly towards the open door. She grabbed him and held him up so that her two friends could see him. 'At least now I can tell you why he's here,' she said. 'I got him during the hols so that he could be my demonstration animal for the holiday project, but I couldn't get him to speak at all. I think it's because he was too big to fit the size criterion. It's such a shame, because he looks so wonderful, especially when he's blundering along – they can move quite fast, you know. I tried the spell *three* times, but I could see it hadn't worked. He just carried on sitting there munching his piece of carrot, looking incredibly dim. I do think tortoises probably *are* incredibly dim. They look as if they only have about one brain cell, so I don't expect he would have had an awful lot to say, but the animals generally say *something*. Even the newt told me he had a bit of a headache – you don't imagine a newt having a headache, do you? Anyway, Speedy just looked completely blank, so either it hadn't worked or he wasn't bright enough to say anything, so I gave up, and then I didn't like to leave him at home, so I brought him with me. You don't believe a word of this, do you?' she added sadly.

Maud and Enid were staring at her

with eyes like saucers.

'Oh, Mil,' said Enid, putting an arm around her fondly. 'I don't know *what* to think this time. Ethel's just so good at everything and you – well, you've never once come up with anything better than Ethel.'

'Especially in the spell department,' agreed Enid.

'But we *know* you wouldn't just tell a huge lie,' added Maud hastily as she saw Mildred's eyes fill with tears.

'Why don't we all have a nice quiet evening and an early night?' suggested Enid. 'Then we can talk it over in the morning.'

'Good idea,' said Maud, sounding rather over-jolly. 'Shall we bring you a plate of supper later on?'

'Don't worry,' said Mildred, trying not to sound hurt. 'I think I'll start my early night right now.'

Enid and Maud slunk out of the room, closing the door quietly behind them.

'I feel *awful*,' said Maud. 'It sounds as if we think she just made it all up – that outburst about the holiday project. We're her *friends*, for goodness' sake. We *ought* to believe her.'

'I know,' said Enid glumly. 'It's difficult sometimes, though, isn't it?'

CHAPTER TEN

A sudden surge of anger swept over Mildred as she sat miserably on the bed, munching the scone/rock cake and contemplating the truly awful treachery of Ethel Hallow.

'It's *so* not fair, Tabs,' she exclaimed to the faithful little cat, who was huddled on her knees. 'No one's ever going to believe my word against Ethel's. She sounds so convincing that even *I* wouldn't believe me if I didn't know! The trouble is that no one else *does* know. No one else was there except you, and you can't speak.'

'*I* can,' said a very small, slightly rasping voice from nowhere.

Mildred jumped. 'Was that you, Tabs?' she breathed.

Tabby purred louder, but said nothing.

'Is someone there?' asked Mildred, looking wildly around the room. 'Where are you?'

'Under the bed,' rasped the reply.

Mildred swung herself on to her knees so that she could look over the side of the bed and see underneath. There she saw the usual pile of boxes and suitcases and Speedy, munching his carrot. 'Was it you?' asked Mildred faintly. 'Did you speak?'

'I did,' said Speedy, turning to face Mildred.

'But – I – how?' gasped Mildred. 'The spell didn't work.'

'It *did* actually,' said Speedy. 'You cast the spell three times and the third time I was so fed up with all your chanting and waving me around in the air that I'd gone inside my shell, which, if you care to fetch a tape measure, fits into a twenty-five-centimetre box with five centimetres to spare at the head or tail end, depending which way you look at it. It *didn't* work when my limbs, tail and head were out, bringing my length to thirty-one centimetres, thereby rendering the spell utterly useless. Not that we tortoises know about anything at *all*, as we are well known to be *incredibly* dim, with possibly only one brain cell.'

Mildred sat back on her heels and gazed at the tortoise, who was gazing back at her with an amused smirk.

'And another thing,' he continued, sounding more grumpy as he went along. 'I suppose you think it's really witty to call a tortoise Speedy when we're not *quite* so fast as, say, a cheetah. Practically everyone calls tortoises some sort of silly name for their own amusement. In fact, I won't say another word unless you can think of a better name for me. I really don't see why I should answer to a name which, frankly, I consider to be an insult.'

So saying, he briskly pulled in his head and front legs, followed by his back legs and tail, and the room fell silent.

'Oh no!' exclaimed Mildred. '*Please* don't go to sleep!'

She groped under the bed, brought him out and laid him carefully on the bedclothes.

'Would you kindly leave me alone,' said the tortoise, sounding coldly polite.

'Look, I'm so sorry about your name,' grovelled Mildred. '*And* about the rude remarks. You're quite right to be offended. I'm *really*, *really* sorry. What sort of name would you like? Is there anything you'd prefer? I mean, I've always wished I was called Miranda, so I do understand.'

'Do you have any famous intelligent people in your world?' asked the tortoise.

'We used to have a famous intelligent man called Einstein,' she said. 'Everyone knows about Einstein.'

'Hmm,' considered the tortoise, half emerging from his shell. 'Einstein. I like it. You can call me Einstein.'

'Brilliant!' said Mildred. 'Einstein. That's *so* much better than – er – the other name.'

'Now, if you don't mind,' said Einstein, 'I'm going to have a nap and I really *don't* want to be disturbed this time. Could you put me back in the cat basket? It's nice and dark in there.'

'Will you have another chat with me soon?' asked Mildred humbly. 'There was something I wanted to ask you.'

'Possibly,' said Einstein. 'Possibly not. Now, if you don't mind, I really am exhausted – and please leave the cat basket door open, as I might want to go for a little walk. Also, tortoises tend to get claustrophobia. Strange, isn't it – when you think how snugly we fit in our shells?'

'Of course! Of course!' agreed Mildred, placing him carefully at the back of the cat basket and wedging the door open with a sock. 'Sleep well – see you later.'

Einstein made no reply, so Mildred clambered back on to her bed with

Tabby, attempting to keep calm as she rummaged through her memory, trying to recollect how many days ago she had cast the spell. To her horror, she suddenly remembered that it had been lunchtime on her aunt's birthday, which gave her the exact date thirteen days ago. This meant that she only had a single day left with Einstein able to speak – only one day before her one witness to the conversation with Ethel fell silent forever.

CHAPTER ELEVEN

The lantern monitor was busily lighting the corridor lanterns as Mildred set off to look for Maud and Enid. They weren't in either of their rooms, so Mildred headed for the yard. During the holidays, Enid had been training her cat to jump from the top of the wall on to her broom as it passed below

at speed. Fortunately for Enid, her cat was a rather bold animal, unlike most cats, who don't usually like fast movement or anything that might be dangerous. For some unknown reason, Stormy really enjoyed this manoeuvre and was happily plummeting off the wall, landing perfectly on the broom, zooming around the yard and leaping back on to the wall, supervised by the proud Enid.

Maud was watching this, hugely impressed.

'Maud! Enid!' yelled Mildred, bounding out of the door and clearing the steps in one leap. 'I've got *proof*! I can prove that Ethel stole my spell!'

'Hang on a minute!' said Enid, calling her broomstick to heel and commanding it to hover while Stormy got her breath back and lay down for a well-deserved washing session.

'Can we go through this tomorrow?' asked Maud, sounding a trifle weary. 'It's been a long day and we've got to go to bed in twenty minutes.'

'There's no time, Maudy,' said Mildred earnestly. 'We've got less than a day to put things right. It's Einstein. He was there all along – and he can speak!'

'Who's Einstein?' exclaimed Maud and Enid together.

'Oh, sorry, I forgot,' laughed Mildred, sounding slightly hysterical. 'It's the

tortoise – he doesn't want to be called Speedy any more. We have to call him Einstein or he won't speak to anyone!'

'What on earth are you on about, Mildred?' asked Maud.

'Come with me,' said Mildred, grabbing Maud's arm. 'The best way is for you to hear him speak too, *then* you'll believe me. I haven't actually asked him if he heard everything when we were all in the tree, or if he saw what happened. Ethel must have knocked my bag out of the tree, although I *thought* it was an accident, but I'm hoping he heard. I'm sure he *must* have done. I know he was awake in the basket when Ethel landed in the tree, because I'd just checked. Come on, it won't take a minute. Come back to my room now and let's ask him together.'

There was no stopping Mildred, who dragged Maud up the steps, followed by Enid, with her broomstick and cat hovering along behind them.

Mildred had left her room door open in her hurry to tell her friends the news about Einstein and when she looked into the cat basket she saw that Einstein had gone. The three friends turned everything upside down searching for him, but it was soon obvious in the sparsely furnished room that he was not there.

'He could be *anywhere*,' said Mildred, standing in the doorway and looking frantically up and down the lantern-lit corridor. 'Perhaps someone's taken him.'

'Let's wait until morning,' said Enid, glancing into the dark doorways of the rooms. 'We've no idea which way he's gone and H.B. will be doing the rounds soon, making sure we're all in bed.'

'But he can't have got far,' wheedled Mildred. 'I was only out of the room for five minutes and he could have tucked himself away *anywhere* by morning.'

'H.B.'s around,' whispered Maud. 'I just know it. The air's gone cold.'

'Good evening, girls,' said Miss Hardbroom's blood-curdling voice as she stepped from the dark area at the top of the stairs.

'Ah, Mildred.' She advanced towards the three friends, who instinctively huddled together. 'I wonder what surprises you're planning for us all tomorrow.'

Nobody spoke and everyone looked at the floor.

'I don't know what you three are up to,' said Miss Hardbroom, 'but I want you all in bed within ten minutes and I don't expect to see you again until assembly tomorrow.'

She vanished silently and the girls stood unmoving for several minutes until the air warmed up.

'It's OK,' said Maud. 'She's gone.'

CHAPTER TWELVE

'Ethel,' whispered Drusilla, tapping on her friend's door and sneaking in just as Ethel was poised to blow out her candle. 'Look what *I* just found coming out of Mildred Hubble's room.'

Ethel sat up in bed and stared in amazement.

'A tortoise!' she laughed. 'What on earth is Mildred Hubble doing with a *tortoise*?'

Drusilla laid Einstein on the bedcover and Ethel held up the candle so they could get a better look at him, but Einstein had completely retreated into his shell and was glowering at them from the depths as if he was hiding inside a dark cave.

'Shall we take it to H.B.?' asked Drusilla. 'You know we're not allowed to have any pets except the cats. She'd probably get *expelled* after the snakes incident and the non-holiday project.'

Ethel sat up in bed, contemplating Mildred's fate. She agreed with Drusilla that it was highly likely that Mildred would be expelled if they took the tortoise to Miss Hardbroom after such a disastrous start to the term – even by Mildred's standards. The trouble was, lessons would be much less fun without the possibility of undermining Mildred Hubble on a daily basis. Ethel didn't see this unpleasant trait as a flaw in her own character; it was just part of life to her, 'getting' Mildred Hubble, and the days would pass more slowly if Mildred wasn't actually there.

'Let's be merciful,' said Ethel jauntily, smiling a regal smile.

'Why?' asked Drusilla, who was every bit as ghastly as Ethel.

'Well,' explained Ethel, 'I am feeling just a *teensy* bit mean about the snakes and the holiday project.'

'But that was just Mildred being an idiot,' exclaimed Drusilla. 'Wasn't it?'

'Not *exactly*,' laughed Ethel. 'I *did* just

sort of try out a snake spell on Mildred's stupid pot and I *did* sort of accidentally-on-purpose knock her bag down the tree when she'd told me all about her "oh so brilliant best idea I've ever had" holiday project. It *was* actually, and as I couldn't think up a project of my own for the first time in my life, I just sort of borrowed it for the time being and replaced it with some of her own plain paper and some nice little smiley faces.'

Drusilla gawped at Ethel, feeling slightly uncomfortable. 'How do you mean *borrowed* it, Eth?' she asked. 'Are you going to give it back?'

'Don't be *dim*, Drusilla,' said Ethel, beginning to be irritated. 'Anyway, I threw Mildred's project into the kitchen bin after I'd brought it up here and copied it out word for word. She'll get over it. It shows she *can* have a good idea. She'll just need to have another

one. Come on, let's take Mr Plod back
to her and make her day.'

No one was in the corridor, but
they could hear voices coming from
Mildred's room, where the door stood
open. Ethel put a finger to her lips
and they crept silently along until they
could hear what was being said. (Ethel
always waited for a few minutes before
she entered a room in case she heard
anything useful.)

On this occasion, she heard something extremely useful.

'*Please*,' Mildred was begging her friends. 'We could meet up after lights out and creep about *very* quietly –'

'We *can't*, Milly,' said Maud, sounding exasperated. 'You *know* we'll get caught.'

Mildred burst into tears. 'You don't *understand*,' she sobbed. 'He's only under the spell for one more day. In fact, not even a whole day. By midday tomorrow the spell will have worn off. It's all my fault. I should have shut my bedroom door and now he's lost and, knowing my luck, we'll find him when he can't speak any more – then *no one* will ever know that Ethel stole my project. He really *can* speak, you know. I had a long conversation with him.'

Ethel made another silencing gesture to Drusilla and motioned her to creep away from the door, back to her room.

Once inside, Ethel closed the door hastily and held up Einstein, who was

so deeply withdrawn into his shell that they couldn't see him at all.

'Who were they on about?' asked Drusilla.

'Our little friend here,' said Ethel. 'Apparently he's not as dense as he looks. Mildred's spell must have worked on him nearly two weeks ago. Now I come to think of it, she *was* hiding something in her cat basket when I met her in the tree and if it was Mr Plod, then he *might* have heard a few things I'd rather he didn't repeat.'

'What shall we do with him, Ethel?' asked Drusilla.

'Easy-peasy,' said Ethel. 'We'll hide him. Mildred said he can speak for another day, but we'll hide him for two, just to be on the safe side. Then we'll get him out and give him back to Mildred as if we've just found him – no harm done either to Mr Plod *or* to me – and Mildred will be grateful just to have him back. You know how ridiculous she is about animals. Only Mildred Hubble could love a tortoise.'

CHAPTER THIRTEEN

Einstein hunched himself
deep within his shell as Ethel
lowered him into a cardboard
box which also contained the
toad that Ethel had used for the animal
spell during Miss Hardbroom's class.
There were airholes punched in the
lid and Einstein emerged from his shell
and stretched his long neck upwards
and tilted his head.

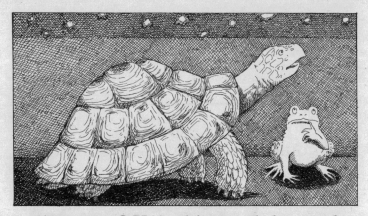

'Are you OK?' whispered the toad.

'Shh,' said Einstein. 'I'm trying to listen.'

Ethel and Drusilla were hatching a plan which involved a very tall pine tree, just outside the school gates, with a hollow near the top, big enough to hide a tortoise in. They were discussing whether to rig up a barrier at the entrance so that he wouldn't fall out. Drusilla was in favour of this, but Ethel wasn't.

'He'll be *fine*. There's no need to make such a fuss. He won't fall out anyway,' she explained to her friend.

'If he really can speak, I'll just tell him not to leave the hollow or he'll smash himself to bits. We'll wait until H.B.'s done her rounds and fly him up there. It'll only take five minutes.'

'Shouldn't we leave him something to eat?' asked Drusilla.

'I suppose so,' said Ethel grudgingly. 'We can pick up some carrots and lettuce from the kitchen dustbins on our way out. You'd better go back to your room now and get some sleep. I'll come and fetch you later on.'

Einstein pulled his head away from the airholes. 'Sorry about that,' he said politely to the toad. 'I just wanted to know what they were going to do with me. I must admit, I *am* petrified of being left on my own at the top of a tree. It goes very badly for tortoises if we drop from a height.'

'What happens if you do?' asked the toad.

'I'd rather not go into details, if you don't mind,' replied Einstein in a quavering voice. 'Let's just say we always avoid being up high. We get claustrophobia too, so a small hollow at the top of a tall tree is just about the worst thing that can happen to a tortoise.'

'Is there anything I can do to help?' asked the toad.

Einstein pondered for a moment.

'Yes, there *is* actually,' he said. 'When this Ethel person takes me to the prison in the sky, I'd like you to set off and find Mildred Hubble's room. It's three doors from here if you turn left, on the other side of the corridor. Tell her that Einstein is in the hollow pine outside the school gates. That way, I might get rescued before there's a gale or some other mishap.'

'I'll *try*,' said the toad. 'Trouble is, I'm not very good at jumping like frogs do.

Perhaps I can lean up against the side of the box so it falls to one side. There's a big enough gap under this door for me to flatten myself and crawl under. Toads are good at flattening. Einstein's a very nice name, by the way. Mine is Cyril.'

'Pleased to meet you, Cyril,' said Einstein.

'Pleased to meet you too,' said the toad, 'and I really will try my best to get assistance if I can possibly manage it.'

CHAPTER FOURTEEN

Along the corridor, Mildred huddled in her bed, listening to the wind rising outside the glassless window. Tabby had burrowed right under the bedclothes to get out of the draught, which was already so strong that Mildred's hair was blowing about on the pillow. She had undone her usual plaits and given the hair a thorough brushing before she'd gone to bed and now it was dancing about all over the place, reminding her of the dreadful occasion last term when she had tried out a regrowth spell and her hair had taken off at such a fantastic speed that it had practically engulfed the whole school.

She sat up in bed and started replaiting it to keep it under control.

'Oh, Tabs,' she said miserably. 'I wonder where on earth Einstein has got to. If I had any idea, I'd go and fetch him, but I haven't a clue.'

Einstein was (just as Ethel had said) in the hollow at the top of the tallest pine outside the school gate.

Ethel hadn't relished the idea of being caught herself, so she had persuaded Drusilla to get dressed again and do the deed in her place. She gave her precise instructions how to creep within the dark shadow of the school, then zoom over the wall and hover up behind the pine trees so she would be covered by the forest. Einstein was in a PE bag across her shoulder underneath her cloak.

He was tempted to try and plead with Drusilla, but he could tell that it would be useless by the way they had talked about him.

Drusilla hovered next to the hollow, which fortunately dropped lower inside than the entrance, lifted Einstein out and placed him in the musty depths with a handful of cabbage leaves and apple peelings.

'Ethel says don't try and get out or you'll fall thirty metres, OK?' said Drusilla helpfully.

Einstein stayed tucked up inside his shell and didn't move.

Drusilla tapped the shell. 'DID YOU HEAR THAT?' she shouted. 'DON'T TRY AND ESCAPE, OR YOU'LL FALL. WE'LL COME AND GET YOU SOON.'

Then she was gone and Einstein was left alone in the pine tree, which was already bending from side to side in a most alarming way.

The minute Ethel had taken Einstein out of the box and crept off to Drusilla's room, Cyril had set to work on his rescue plan. Fortunately, the lid of the box was not very tight-fitting and he found that he could dislodge it by jumping a short distance and bashing it with his head – like heading a football. Then it

was quite easy to stand on tiptoe and jump enough to land half-and-half on the top edge and slither down the other side. The box was on the bedside locker, which was quite a height from the floor, but Cyril aimed for Ethel's school bag, which broke his fall. After that he was soon squeezing himself flat underneath the door and out into the shadowy corridor.

'So far, so good!' he thought proudly.

Mildred had finished replaiting her hair, moved her bed away from the window in case of rain and snuggled right under the bedcovers. The wind outside had begun to roar and moan in the pine trees, sounding like a stormy sea. She was so far down the bed that she didn't hear the tiny sound of a toad flapping his feet against the heavy wooden door. Cyril was outside, tapping as hard as he could with a back and front foot. He had tried to squeeze underneath, but the space was far smaller than the gap below Ethel's door.

'Excuse me!' he called out in his tiny toad voice.

Fortunately, cats can detect the very smallest sound and movement. Tabby wriggled out from the bedclothes and

rushed over to the crack beneath the door, where he started scrabbling with his paw.

Mildred got out of bed and lit her candle. 'What is it, Tab?' she asked. 'Is someone there? Is it Einstein?'

She opened the door and saw Cyril, still with his front and back leg upraised to continue his attempt at knocking.

'Oh, hello!' he said, relieved to see her. 'Are you Mildred Hubble?'

Mildred bent down and picked up the little toad very carefully.

'I am,' she whispered.

'Brilliant!' said Cyril. 'I'm Cyril. I was Ethel Hallow's demonstration toad in the potion lab today. I've brought you a message from Einstein.'

CHAPTER FIFTEEN

Mildred sat on her bed, listening to the message from her lost tortoise with a sinking heart.

'Are you *sure* she took him all the way up there?' she asked, clutching at straws. 'Perhaps she just put him in a cupboard in Drusilla's room?'

'No, it was the hollow pine outside the school gates,' insisted Cyril. 'She was really definite about it.'

'But it's about thirty metres high!' said Mildred. 'The other trees are really tall anyway, but that one's a good three metres above the others.'

She closed her eyes, imagining going out on a rescue mission on such an awful night when five minutes ago she had been tucked up with Tabby, thinking how nice it felt to be safe and warm inside.

'He's terrified of heights,' continued Cyril relentlessly. 'He might fall out and the wind's getting worse. I think there's going to be a storm.'

As if to underline his words, the wind rose to a screaming pitch and a squall of rain suddenly lashed against the castle walls, spraying an arc of drops through the narrow window.

'He really *is* scared,' said Cyril. 'His voice went all wobbly when he told me where they were taking him. I promised I'd ask you to help. *Will* you help?'

'Of course I will,' said Mildred, trying hard to sound confident and capable. 'I'll just fetch my broom.'

Tabby burrowed back under the

covers at the mention of the word 'broom'. Mildred sat on the edge of the bed and stroked him reassuringly.

'It's OK, Tab,' she said gently. 'This is an illegal mission, so you're excused broomstick duty tonight.' She turned to the toad. 'Where would you like to go, Cyril, now that your task is done?'

'Could you pop me back outside the school gates?' said Cyril. 'Then I can make my way down through the forest. I *love* this sort of weather actually. It's very good for the complexion.'

Mildred glanced at the toad's dry and knobbly skin and stifled a giggle.

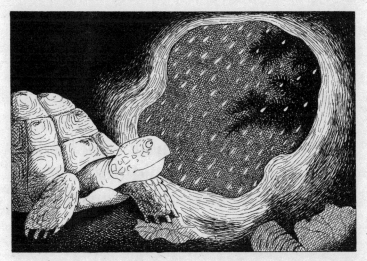

Up in the hollow pine, Einstein was trying hard not to panic. The wind had set up a constant moan, with sudden bursts of extra force that felt as if they would snap the already weak and hollowed tree in two.

'She isn't going to come,' thought Einstein dismally. 'The whole tree will disintegrate and I'll be smashed into tiny pieces.'

He tried keeping himself tightly hidden inside his shell, but the horrible noise outside was so frightening that he couldn't stop himself coming out to check. The darkness all around him and the rain spraying in through the entrance made him feel even worse, so he retreated inside his shell – then he came out again – then he went back in again. In the end he did this so many times that he was beside himself with exhausted confusion.

'*Please* come and get me out of here, Mildred Hubble,' he said desperately. '*Please.*'

Mildred was doing her best. She had decided not to involve Maud or Enid this time. When she imagined waking Maud up and announcing that she needed help rescuing an escaped tortoise from the top of the tallest pine tree in the forest in the middle of a gale, she could hear how ridiculous it sounded.

'No, Mildred,' she said to herself.

'You're on your own with this one.'

The summer dress was too flimsy for an adventure like this, so Mildred put her school cardigan on over her pyjamas to keep a bit warmer and tucked the trouser ends into her socks. She wrapped her cloak around her, tied it in the middle with her school sash to stop it blowing about and set off to the schoolyard, the toad in one hand and her trusty broom in the other.

When she reached the side door, which was smaller and easier to unbolt, she was suddenly struck with terror as she looked out into the rain-swept noisy darkness. Mildred was afraid of the dark – a most embarrassing problem for a trainee witch – and it didn't get much darker and more frightening than the night waiting for her outside.

'He must be petrified all the way up there,' said Cyril, as if reading her thoughts. 'Just put me down here if you like. It's only a short hop to the gates and there's a ten-centimetre gap for me to squeeze under.'

'All right,' said Mildred. 'Thank you so much for telling me where he is. I'm sure we'll be OK once I've found the tree.'

For a mad moment, she wondered if she might ask Cyril to come with her for company as she watched him hop and flop down the steps and disappear into the storm.

'What am I thinking about?' she asked herself. 'Making friends with a toad! It's funny how perfectly he speaks English, though. I wonder if I lived in a different country, would the toad speak in that language? And does the spell adapt to any language in the world? Perhaps I've discovered an international spell. Mildred Hubble, international spell-maker!'

At that moment a gust of wind banged the door loudly back against the inside corridor. Mildred grabbed it and waited nervously, straining her ears to hear if anyone had noticed, but no one came. She decided to take a lantern from the corridor and tie it on to the front of her broom to light her way. The only thing to use was her sash, which she took from her waist, causing the cloak to billow out around her.

'OK, broom,' she said, trying to

sound like a person in charge. 'Hover. That's right!'

Mildred stepped outside, with the broom doing its best to keep steady in the gusting wind.

The door slammed deafeningly shut behind her. 'Can't be helped,' thought Mildred desperately as she arranged herself side-saddle on the broom and tucked her cloak firmly underneath her. 'OK, little broom. Up, up, up and over the wall.'

CHAPTER SIXTEEN

Miss Hardbroom was having a late-evening cup of hot chocolate with Miss Cackle in Miss Cackle's study.

'There's a door banging downstairs somewhere,' said Miss Cackle, offering Miss Hardbroom a biscuit from a large tin. 'Sounds like a nasty storm's brewing out there.'

'Very nasty,' agreed Miss Hardbroom, taking a custard cream and resting it in her saucer. 'I was just wondering, Miss Cackle, how much longer we have to *plough on* trying to educate Mildred Hubble in this establishment.'

'Why?' asked Miss Cackle, looking up from the tin, where she was trying to decide whether to take a chocolate biscuit or a pink wafer, or maybe both. 'What's she done *now*?'

'*Everything*,' said Miss Hardbroom wearily. 'It would take all night to list the events and we've only been back for one day. I don't think I have the *stamina* to struggle through the entire term trying to keep Mildred Hubble in some sort of order. I honestly don't know how she does it – she's a sort of trouble magnet.'

'But rather sweet, don't you think?' said Miss Cackle with a fond smile. 'Always considering others and such

a good owner to that hopeless cat of hers.'

'That's all very well,' said Miss Hardbroom crisply. 'But having a rather sweet nature doesn't necessarily equip a girl to be a suitable pupil at this school – the finest witches' academy for miles around.'

'The *only* witches' academy for miles around,' laughed Miss Cackle, attempting to inject a little humour before her colleague plunged into an endless list of Mildred's faults.

'What's that?' asked Miss Hardbroom, suddenly peering out of the window.

'What's *what*?' asked Miss Cackle,

getting up reluctantly from her comfortable armchair.

'Look,' said Miss Hardbroom. 'There's a light flickering over there.'

'Where, Miss Hardbroom?' said Miss Cackle. 'I can't see anything.'

'Just outside the gates,' said Miss Hardbroom. 'It's disappeared now – no, there it is, higher up. It looks like a giant firefly.'

'We don't *have* any giant fireflies, do we?' asked Miss Cackle hopefully.

'They don't actually exist, Miss Cackle,' said Miss Hardbroom witheringly. 'I'd better go and check.'

'Surely not, Miss Hardbroom!' exclaimed Miss Cackle. 'You mustn't go out there on such a night. I'm sure it's nothing.'

'It looks like a definite *something* to me,' said Miss Hardbroom sternly. 'It keeps disappearing and then reappearing several metres higher up. Definitely "something" enough to investigate.'

CHAPTER SEVENTEEN

Mildred was hovering her way very slowly and carefully up towards the top of the trees outside the school gates. She couldn't tell which one was the hollow pine yet, but figured that she might be able to see it by its extra height when she reached the very top. She knew it was right in front of the gates, which was a help. The wind was especially ferocious this far up, getting stronger the higher she rose, and the valiant broomstick kept lurching every time it was hit by a particularly strong gust or a cannon-burst of rain. Mildred's unsecured cloak didn't help, billowing like a sail or suddenly twisting above her like a faulty parachute.

Every now and then, she ducked behind the front row of trees and held on to a branch to have a rest, out of the full force of the storm. The trouble was that if you tried to hover behind the first row of trees, you were blown into the ones behind, which grew very close together. The best way to ascend was, unfortunately, out in the open, even though it was very difficult to keep your balance.

During one such rest, gasping to get her breath back, Mildred suddenly felt a glow of pride that she was able to control a broomstick in these freak conditions.

'It's funny what you can do when it's

an emergency,' she thought. 'Better get going again before my luck runs out.'

'Einstein!' she called. 'Einstein! Where are you?' But the wind whisked her voice away like thistledown.

Einstein was trying very hard (and not succeeding) to pull himself together. His head, legs and tail were zooming in and out of his shell like an insane cuckoo clock and he was muttering to himself, attempting to take his mind off the fact that the tree was now making ominous deep creaking sounds.

When he saw the flickering light from Mildred's broom outside the entrance to the hollow, he thought it was lightning and this was the very last straw. Yelling one last desperate 'HELP!', he pulled himself back into the deepest depths of his shell and switched off.

'Einstein?!' yelled Mildred, just catching the 'Help!' above the lashing rain. 'Where are you?'

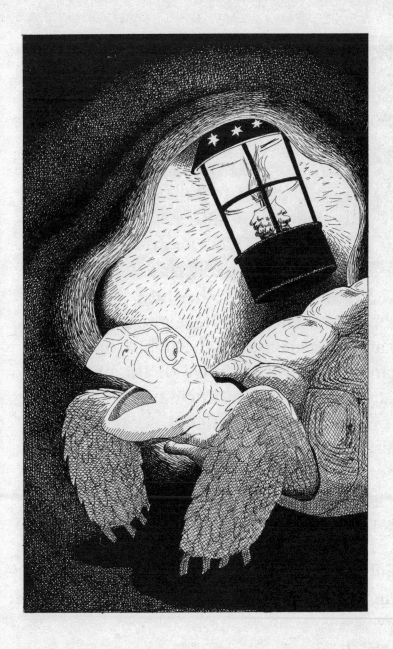

Mildred wobbled her way towards the place where she thought the voice had come from and the light from the lantern caught the edge of the hollow. She flew to the entrance and hung on to the scrubby branches so that the lantern lit up the inside of the hollow and Einstein's closed-up shell.

'It's all right, Einstein!' Mildred exclaimed. 'I'm here! I'll have to button you inside my cardigan so you don't fall. Don't be scared. I'll hold you very tightly. I won't let you fall.'

Steadying herself by clutching the edge of the hollow with one hand, she gently lifted the terrified tortoise out with the other and peered into the deep cave-like area at the front of his shell, where he had retracted himself so far that he was invisible.

'Say something, Einsy,' she said affectionately, buttoning him tightly inside her cardigan in case the exhausted broomstick lurched in the wind and threw them both off. 'You're safe now. I'll have you down in a jiffy. We'll be back in the warm before you know it.'

CHAPTER EIGHTEEN

Going down was so much more pleasant than going up, as the wind diminished in strength towards the forest floor. Mildred breathed a sigh of relief when her feet bounced on the grass and she could finally stand upright again, although she felt slightly unsteady, rather like the feeling you have when you've been on a boat for a long time and finally reach land.

'Come on, Einstein,' she said, peering down the front of her cardigan. 'Speak to me! You're OK now, we're on planet Earth again. Isn't this just my luck. The best broomstick-handling I've ever done and no one to witness it.'

'Just one witness, Mildred Hubble,' said the most unwelcome voice that Mildred could possibly hear.

'Miss Hardbroom!' exclaimed Mildred, jumping right off her feet in horrified surprise as she saw her form mistress, wrapped in a sodden cloak,

standing close behind her, holding up a lantern. 'Oh, Miss Hardbroom, I know this looks bad, but –'

'Spare me the sound of your voice for a few minutes, Mildred,' said Miss Hardbroom, smoothing back a tendril of dripping hair. 'Let's get out of this wind before you launch into the usual raving explanation of your tiresome behaviour. Miss Cackle is waiting in her study.'

Miss Cackle was just making a second cup of hot chocolate when her study door crashed open and a dripping Miss Hardbroom swept in, guiding the drenched Mildred in front of her.

'Oh, my goodness!' exclaimed Miss Cackle. 'Miss Hardbroom, Mildred, come over here and stand by the fire. Mildred, take off that wet cloak and cardigan at once! Miss Hardbroom, please remove your cloak and get yourself warm. You'll both catch pneumonia in all those wet things.'

Mildred wrestled her way out of the cloak, which had twisted itself like a scarf around her shoulders, and began, very carefully, to unbutton her cardigan. Miss Cackle was watching her intently, waiting to take the wet garments and drape them near the fire, so there was no hiding Einstein, who was still lurking deep inside his shell.

'Good gracious me!' said Miss Cackle. 'Is that a *tortoise*, Mildred?'

'Yes, Miss Cackle,' said Mildred bleakly. 'He's called Einstein. He can speak, Miss Cackle, but he's been so upset being up in the tree that I think he's gone into his shell – if you see what I mean – with the shock of it all. Tortoises are really afraid of heights and they have terrible claustrophobia, so it's no wonder he's in shock.'

'How did he get up the tree in the first place, Mildred?' asked Miss Hardbroom in a matter-of-fact voice. 'They don't fly – as well as having claustrophobia and a fear of heights – do they? Or is this just another little-known fact about tortoises that only *you* are privileged to know?'

'Someone took him up there, Miss Hardbroom,' said Mildred.

'Do you happen to know who that someone was, Mildred?' asked Miss Cackle.

'I think it was Ethel Hallow, Miss

Cackle,' said Mildred miserably.

'And how do you *know* it was Ethel?' asked Miss Hardbroom.

'Her toad told me,' said Mildred, realizing how mad this sounded. 'You know, the one she used today in potions. He's called Cyril. He could speak, so he hopped along to tell me what had happened. He knocked on the door with his feet and –'

'So where is the toad now, Mildred?' asked Miss Hardbroom.

'I let him go,' said Mildred, 'in the yard. They don't mind the rain – in fact, they actually prefer it – and he wanted to go home.'

Miss Hardbroom stared in wonder, first at Mildred and then at Miss Cackle. 'Where did the tortoise come from, Mildred?' asked Miss Cackle, looking totally baffled.

'I think this is going to be a very long story, Headmistress,' said Miss Hardbroom. 'I'll take charge of the traumatized tortoise for the night and we can assemble the relevant pupils and the tortoise at some point tomorrow. Not Cyril, though – a pity, as I'm sure he could fill us in on several important details.'

'Could I keep Einstein with me, Miss Hardbroom?' asked Mildred desperately. 'He still hasn't come out of his shell and I'm really worried about him.'

'He'll be quite safe with me, Mildred,' said Miss Hardbroom. 'You may take a hot bath to warm yourself up, but be quick about it.'

'Could we have the meeting early, Miss Hardbroom?' asked Mildred. 'It's just that the spell only works until noon and he won't be able to speak again after that.'

Miss Hardbroom held the shell up and looked into the dark interior, where Einstein's front legs were pulled in tightly to shield him from view.

'Are you *sure* he can speak, Mildred?' she asked.

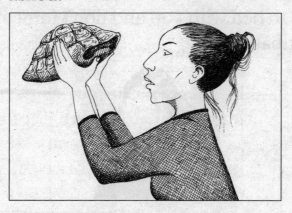

'Perhaps he's hibernating,' said Miss Cackle brightly.

'They're just coming *out* of hibernation at this time of year, Miss Cackle,' said Miss Hardbroom waspishly. 'Tomorrow morning then, Mildred, before assembly.'

'Oh, thank you *so* much, Miss Hardbroom,' said Mildred gratefully, 'and please could you put him somewhere nice and warm. They hate the cold and he's had such a terrible time.'

'I do know a *little* bit about tortoises, Mildred,' said Miss Hardbroom. 'Now off to bed with you and don't forget the hot bath.'

CHAPTER NINETEEN

Bright and early next morning, there was a tap on Mildred's door while she was still getting dressed, ready to go down to breakfast.

Mildred opened the door and found a nervous-looking first-year named Mavis standing outside.

'What is it?' asked Mildred, trying to sound kindly. The first-years looked so small and shy and Mildred remembered only too well what that felt like.

'I've brought a message from Miss Hardbroom,' said Mavis. 'She wants to see you in Miss Cackle's study right away.'

'OK, Mave,' said Mildred. 'Message received. Off you go – and ask Maud to save me some toast, would you?'

'Of course!' replied Mavis proudly, glad to be of assistance to Mildred Hubble, whose adventures were legendary throughout the school.

Mildred brushed and replaited her hair as tightly as possible and smoothed her dress, hoping to make a good impression from the first moment of what could prove to be a very difficult interview.

Mildred knocked firmly on Miss Cackle's door.

'Come in, Mildred,' said Miss Cackle, beckoning her inside. 'Take a seat.'

Mildred was the last to arrive. Miss Cackle and Miss Hardbroom were already seated on one side of the desk and Ethel was sitting bolt upright on the other, looking annoyed. Einstein, still invisible inside his shell, had been placed in Miss Cackle's overflowing in-

tray, which made rather a comfortable nest for him.

'Now then, girls,' continued Miss Cackle. 'Let's try and get to the bottom of the extraordinary story which Mildred began last night. Mildred, would you like to tell Ethel what you said to us yesterday, when Miss Hardbroom brought you in from the storm?'

Ethel's eyes had narrowed into slits, but Mildred took a deep breath and began.

'I had to rescue Einstein – that's my tortoise's name – from the hollow pine, Ethel,' she said firmly. 'Your toad – you know, the one you used to demonstrate *my* spell, the spell you stole from me – well, your toad came with a message that you'd hidden Einstein up in the hollow pine tree and he asked me to go and get him. So I did. That's all really.'

'*All?*' thundered Miss Hardbroom. 'That sounds like a very long list of accusations to me, Mildred. Well, Ethel, what do you have to say?'

'I'm stunned, Miss Hardbroom,' exclaimed Ethel. 'I don't know *what* she's talking about. I certainly didn't go *anywhere* last night, I was fast asleep in bed, and I *never* stole her spell. Why on earth would I want to steal a spell from Mildred Hubble? You'd have to be mad to steal a spell from *her*. It'd probably turn you into a cockroach or something. I don't know how to convince you, Miss Hardbroom – I definitely didn't go out last night. If someone put him there, it certainly wasn't me!'

There was silence for a few moments while everyone looked at each other, then Miss Cackle spoke.

'Well, if you didn't, Ethel,' she asked, 'who did?'

'I think you'll find that her name was Drusilla,' said a small, rasping voice.

Everyone jumped as they saw that Einstein had emerged from his shell and was blundering through the papers to the edge of the in-tray.

'Einstein!' exclaimed Mildred joyfully. 'You've come out! Are you all right?'

'Yes, yes,' said the little tortoise, stretching his long neck and all four legs one after the other. 'Don't fuss. I was just a bit upset last night and thought I'd take a *very* long nap. Now then, my friend, what would you like to know?'

'Everything really,' said Mildred. 'From when you wandered out of my bedroom till I found you in the hollow tree.'

'Was it you who rescued me?' asked Einstein. 'I wondered how I got back down here again. It was such a horrible night and I was so scared. Thank you *so* much. Well, let me think. Oh yes, I went for a walk and Drusilla found me and took me to Ethel's room. Ethel was just bringing me back to you when she overheard you and your friends saying that I could talk, so she told Drusilla that she was going to hide me up in the pine until the speaking-spell ran out. She *was* going to give me back to you after that, I remember her saying.'

'Can you remember anything else?' asked Mildred hopefully. 'Do you remember what Ethel and I talked about when we were sitting in that tree on our way to school?'

'I *don't* remember that,' said Einstein. 'But I *do* remember what she said to Drusilla in her bedroom. She said that she knocked your bag down the tree on purpose and she borrowed your project and that she threw it into the kitchen bin after she'd copied it out – oh yes, and she said something about trying out a snake spell on your pot. She didn't seem to want to go out on such an awful night, so she talked Drusilla into it instead. But it was Ethel's idea, she made Drusilla do it. Anything else you'd like to know?'

CHAPTER TWENTY

Down in the yard behind the kitchen, standing next to the huge bin, which had been turned on its side, Miss Cackle, Miss Hardbroom and Mildred watched as Ethel sifted through old bits of pie and custard and a mass of burnt porridge, still warm from the cauldron when the cooks had prepared breakfast.

'Keep looking, Ethel,' said Miss Hardbroom menacingly. 'We're going to turn over every old tea bag, every fish skin, until we find Mildred's project.'

Ethel sat back on her heels, looking desperate.

'It's not *fair*, Miss Hardbroom,' she said. 'I don't know how you can believe the word of a *tortoise* against mine.'

'There it is!' exclaimed Mildred, diving into a pile of incinerated toast. 'I can see it! It's my handwriting, look!'

Mildred held up her project, tea-stained and damp, but still recognizable as her treasured work.

Miss Hardbroom took it from her with one finger and thumb and looked at it sideways. 'Well, well,' she said coolly to Ethel. '*I* never thought that I would take the word of a tortoise above yours, Ethel, but it would seem that he is the more honest of the two of you. Now then, Ethel, before you try and wriggle out of this, let me ask you: did you steal Mildred's project, did you turn Mildred's pot into a snake and did you ask Drusilla to imprison this poor creature at the top of the hollow pine? Take your time, Ethel. I want a truthful answer from you.'

163

Ethel knew that she was cornered and in the worst trouble she'd ever been, with no way out.

'I did everything, Miss Hardbroom,' she muttered. 'The snake pot, the project, and I got Drusilla to hide the tortoise because he knew too much. I'm sorry I lied. I'm sorry about everything.'

Maud and Enid were in the middle of breakfast when Mildred dashed in to join them. She was glowing from head to foot and smiling so broadly that it looked as if her head might fall off.

'What's happened, Millie?' asked Maud, passing her the two slices of toast that they'd kept for her. 'You look as if you might go into orbit.'

'Oh, it's wonderful, Maud,' said Mildred. 'Ethel's actually confessed to H.B. and Miss Cackle that she stole my project. She'd thrown it into the kitchen bin and H.B. made her look through all the slimy rubbish till she found it. Then she confessed that she'd turned my pot into rattlesnakes *and* she admitted that she'd got Drusilla to hide Einstein up the tree last night –'

'Up what tree?' asked Enid.

'Oh, I forgot,' said Mildred. 'All that happened while you were asleep. I'll tell you about it later. I'll just stuff down this toast or I'll be starving at assembly.'

CHAPTER TWENTY-ONE

Miss Cackle and Miss Hardbroom stood on the platform with the other teachers, looking down on the girls as they ploughed through their daily rendition of the school song.

As the last notes faded away, Miss Cackle stepped forward and smiled at her flock. 'Good morning, girls,' she said fondly, 'and what a good morning it is indeed for Mildred Hubble. Step up here, Mildred – and Ethel Hallow. I think Ethel has something important to say to you, Mildred.'

Mildred and Ethel both looked at the floor as they made their way up the steps to stand under the steely gaze of Miss Hardbroom: Ethel wishing the ground would swallow her up, caught out in such a torrent of lies; Mildred self-conscious as she felt hundreds of pairs of eyes watching her curiously.

'Various unpleasant events have happened since the beginning of this term,' announced Miss Hardbroom, 'and the evidence unfortunately pointed to Mildred Hubble as the culprit. I have to tell you all that Mildred was entirely innocent of any blame whatsoever. Not only has she written the best holiday project that I have ever seen, she also carried out the heroic rescue of a poor dumb animal – well, not so dumb actually – in the middle of a virtual hurricane.

'Ethel Hallow took Mildred's spell and passed it off as her own. I'm not surprised that you wanted it, Ethel, but you can't just take something that doesn't belong to you, nor must you use spell-making to wreck the work of someone who is better than you in that subject. I think an apology is in order, Ethel.'

'Sorry, Mildred,' mumbled Ethel, staring at her shoes.

'Louder please, Ethel,' said Miss Hardbroom. 'So that the whole school can hear.'

'Sorry, Mildred,' said Ethel in a strangled voice. 'It was a brilliant spell – the best idea ever. I wish it really had been mine.'

'Thanks, Ethel,' said Mildred shyly, pleased that Ethel had admitted everything, however grudgingly. 'I'm sure you'll think up one of your own in no time.'

After assembly, there was a double broomstick lesson in the yard for Form Three, which took them right up to lunchtime.

'You must be *so* pleased, Millie,' said Maud, flinging an arm around Mildred's shoulder as the lunch-bell rang out. 'Everything's turned out *so* well and the one thing H.B. can't stand is dishonesty, so Ethel's *really* got to watch out now or *she'll* be for the chop.'

'I know,' said Mildred, smiling, 'and Miss Cackle felt so sorry for me about the snake-pot incident after I'd done so well that she's going to let us have a proper craft room with a kiln and everything. But the best thing of all is that I get to keep Einstein as an extra pet – Einstein!' She dropped her broomstick with a clatter and raced for the door into school.

'What's the matter, Mil?' yelled Enid.

'It's twelve o'clock!' Mildred called back. 'I won't have time to have a last chat with him before the spell breaks!'

Mildred leapt up the front steps, dashed along the corridor and up the spiral staircase two steps at a time. She whirled into her room and lay down flat on the floor so she could see Einstein, who was sitting happily in the open doorway of the cat basket under her bed.

'Einstein,' said Mildred softly, 'can you still speak? Say something, please.'

'I'm glad I belong to you,' said Einstein, speaking for the last time in his rasping little voice. Then he picked up his carrot and began munching it, gazing vacantly into space and looking for all the world like a tortoise with only one brain cell.

'And I'm glad you're mine,' said Mildred, smoothing his knobbly shell. 'You too!' she added, laughing as Tabby landed on her back, miaowing loudly. She felt the same sudden surge of hope that she had felt the day before, when everything had looked so promising. 'Perhaps it *is* going to be a brilliant term after all.'

Mildred Hubble is always getting her spells
wrong at Miss Cackle's Academy for Witches.
But she manages to get by until she turns Ethel,
the teacher's pet, into her deadly enemy . . .

The first in the much-loved Worst Witch series

puffin.co.uk

What happens when disaster-prone
Mildred Hubble meets new girl Enid Nightshade?

*She may be the worst witch at Miss Cackle's Academy
for Witches, but she's the best friend you could ever have!*

A new term, and Mildred is determined to lose her reputation as the worst witch Miss Cackle's Academy has ever seen – but things get rapidly out of hand.

Millions of readers love Mildred Hubble – and so will you . . .

Mildred stows away her beloved cat, Tabby, on a class trip to the seaside. Trying to keep him out of sight of Miss Hardbroom leads her from one disaster to another, and soon she really is all at sea.

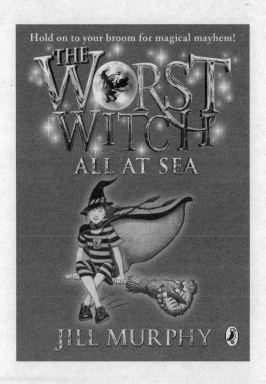

'Hurray for Jill Murphy . . . girls will love the antics of Mildred Hubble and her hopeless tabby cat' – *Independent*

puffin.co.uk

A new teacher, a hair-growth spell gone wrong and a cat who refuses to fly – can Mildred overcome all obstacles and save the day?

'A lovely, sparkly book' – *Observer*

puffin.co.uk

Winter Term starts surprisingly well for
Mildred Hubble. But when she sees a wishing star
things quickly take an unexpected turn.
Can she put things right or does this latest
disaster spell the end for the Worst Witch?

'Millions of young readers have fallen under the
spell of Jill Murphy's Worst Witch' – *Sunday Express*

puffin.co.uk

It all started with a Scarecrow

Puffin is over seventy years old.

Sounds ancient, doesn't it? But Puffin has never been
so lively. We're always on the lookout for the next big
idea, which is how it began all those years ago.

Penguin Books was a big idea from the mind of
a man called Allen Lane, who in 1935 invented
the quality paperback and changed the world.
**And from great Penguins, great Puffins grew,
changing the face of children's books forever.**

The first four Puffin Picture Books were hatched in 1940 and the
first Puffin story book featured a man with broomstick arms called
Worzel Gummidge. In 1967 Kaye Webb, Puffin Editor, started the
Puffin Club, promising to **'make children into readers'**.
She kept that promise and over 200,000 children became devoted
Puffineers through their quarterly instalments of *Puffin Post*.

Many years from now, we hope you'll look back and
remember Puffin with a smile. **No matter what your age
or what you're into, there's a Puffin for everyone.**
The possibilities are endless, but one thing is for sure:
whether it's a picture book or a paperback, a sticker book
or a hardback, **if it's got that little Puffin
on it – it's bound to be good.**